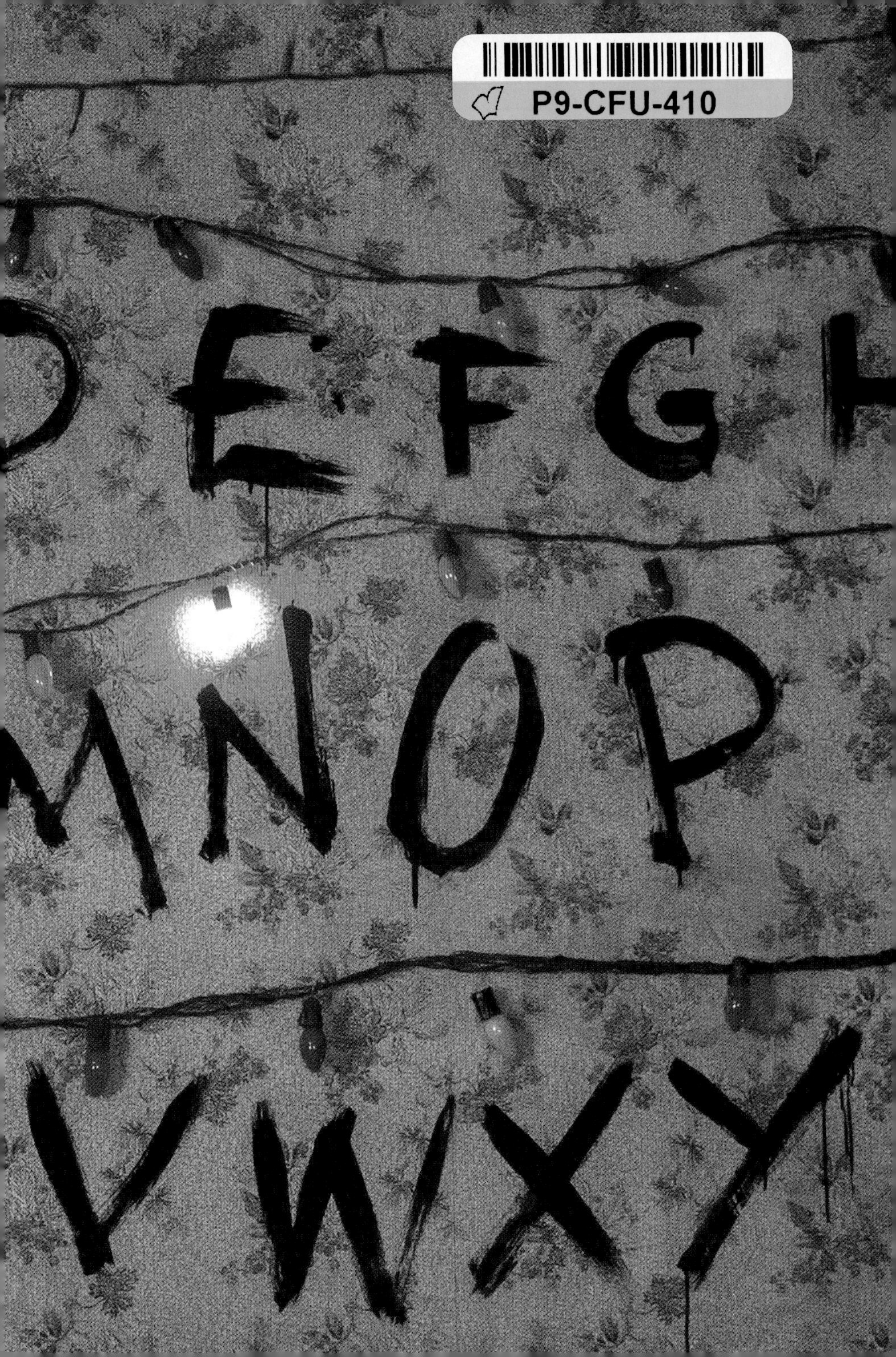
E F G
M N O P
V W X Y

Published in the United States by Random House Children's Books, a division of Penguin Random House LLC, New York.
Random House and the colophon are registered trademarks of Penguin Random House LLC. *Stranger Things* and all related titles, characters, and logos are trademarks of Netflix Inc. Created by The Duffer Brothers.

Images on pages 11 (bottom right), 12 (bottom left), 16-17, 22, 28–29, 38 (bottom left), 69, and 78 (bottom left) are used under license from Shutterstock.com.

rhcbooks.com

Library of Congress Cataloging-in-Publication Data is available upon request.

ISBN 978-1-9848-5195-6 (trade)—ISBN 978-1-9848-5196-3 (ebook)

Printed in the United States of America
10 9 8 7 6 5 4 3 2 1

First Edition

HOW TO SURVIVE IN A STRANGER THINGS WORLD

Compiled by Matthew J. Gilbert

Random House New York

NO PLACE LIKE HOME

WELCOME
TO
HAWKINS

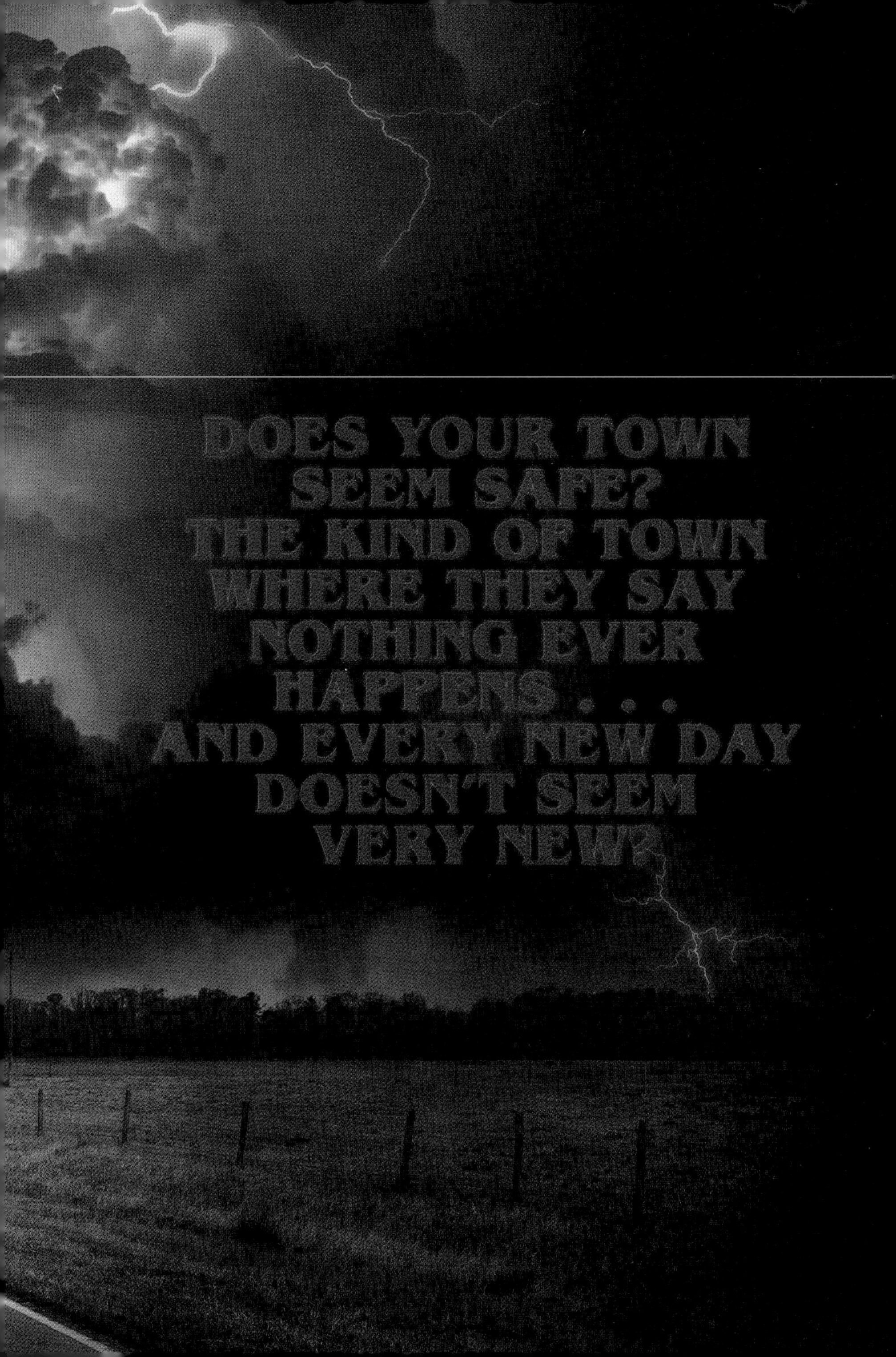
DOES YOUR TOWN SEEM SAFE?
THE KIND OF TOWN WHERE THEY SAY NOTHING EVER HAPPENS . . .
AND EVERY NEW DAY DOESN'T SEEM VERY NEW?

POLICE

Mornings are for
COFFEE
&
CONTEMPLATION.

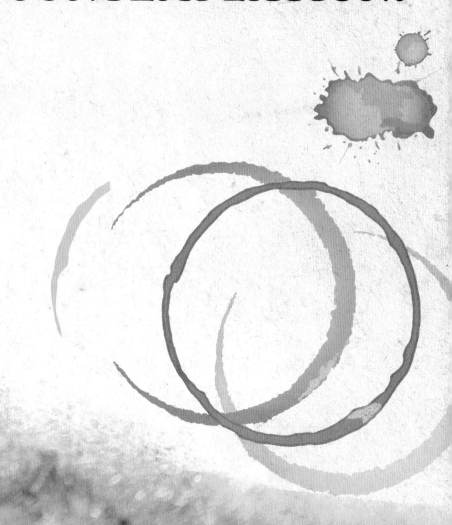

WAFFLES
ARE GOOD
anytime.

SCHOOL CAN MAKE YOU

FEEL LIKE A STRANGER.

If you want to fit in, you need to look cool—especially your hair.

Use the shampoo
and conditioner.

And when your hair's damp,
not wet, okay?

When it's damp,
you do four puffs of the
Farrah Fawcett spray.

Always be READY for a CURIOSITY voyage.

And hold on to your CURIOSITY PADDLES.

SOME
CURIOSITY
DOORS
SHOULD
STAY
LOCKED.

And when in doubt,

roll the dice.

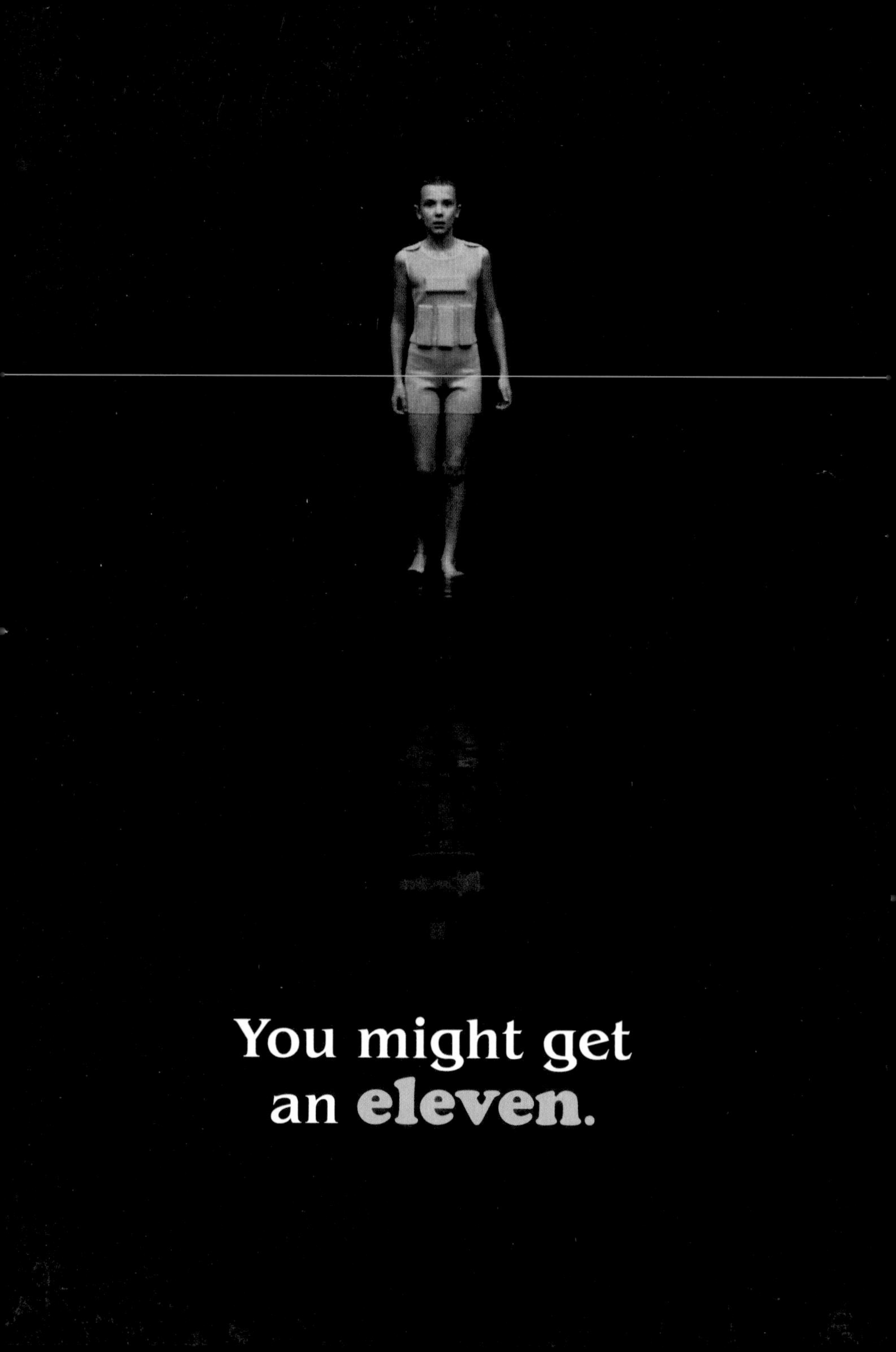
You might get
an eleven.

Dare to be
BITCHIN'

FRIENDS DON'T LIE

Friends
find adventure
everywhere.

Whether
it's in a
basement . . .

. . . OR ON THE
DARKEST EDGES
OF TOWN.

A FRIEND has your back

when things get ROCKY.

"OUR FRIEND HAS SUPERPOWERS, AND SHE SQUEEZED YOUR TINY BLADDER WITH HER MIND!"

Did you know
a stranger is
just a friend
you haven't
met?

Or they could be
a government
agent sent to
silence you.

Someone who cares ALWAYS gets you.

They JUST do.

"If we're both going crazy,

then we'll go crazy
together, right?"

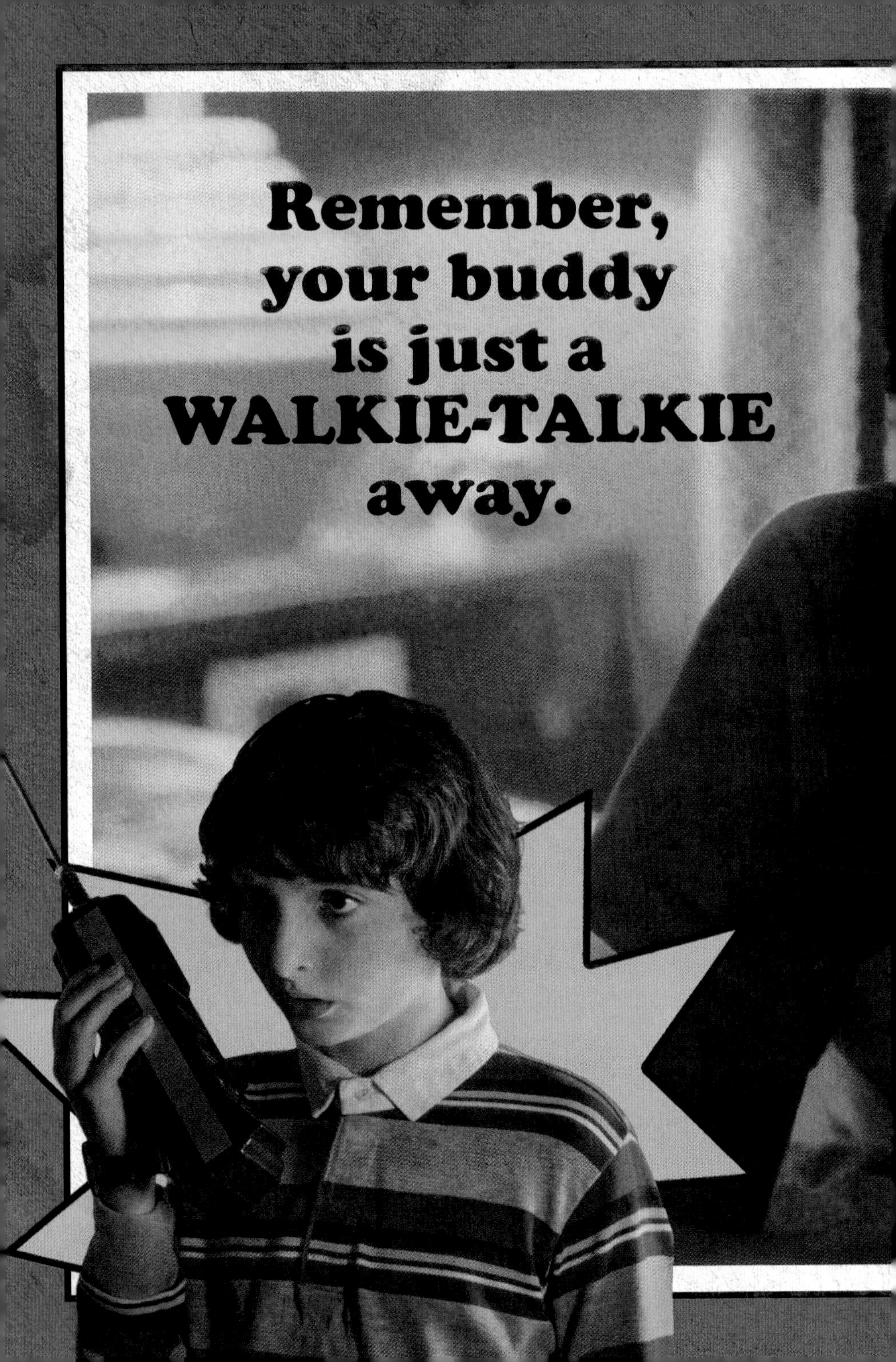
Remember, your buddy is just a WALKIE-TALKIE away.

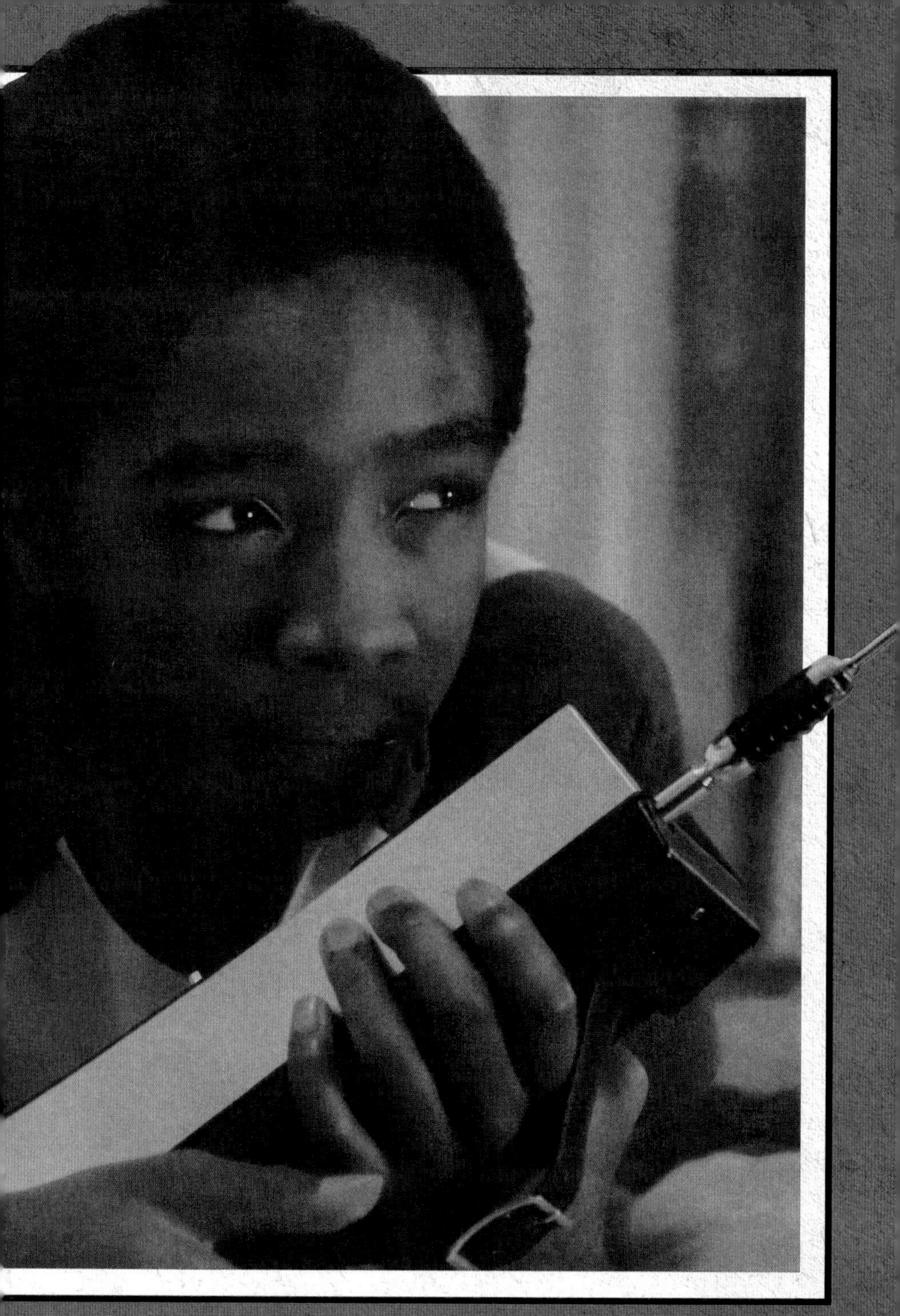

But be careful
not to say
too much.

It's called code

SHUT
YOUR
MOUTH.

Sadly,
some friends
grow apart.

HAWKINS HIGH SCHOOL
GO TIGERS!
Some friends
VANISH
FOREVER.

THE UPSIDE DOWN

Sometimes you see something STRANGE

WELCOME
TO
HAWKINS

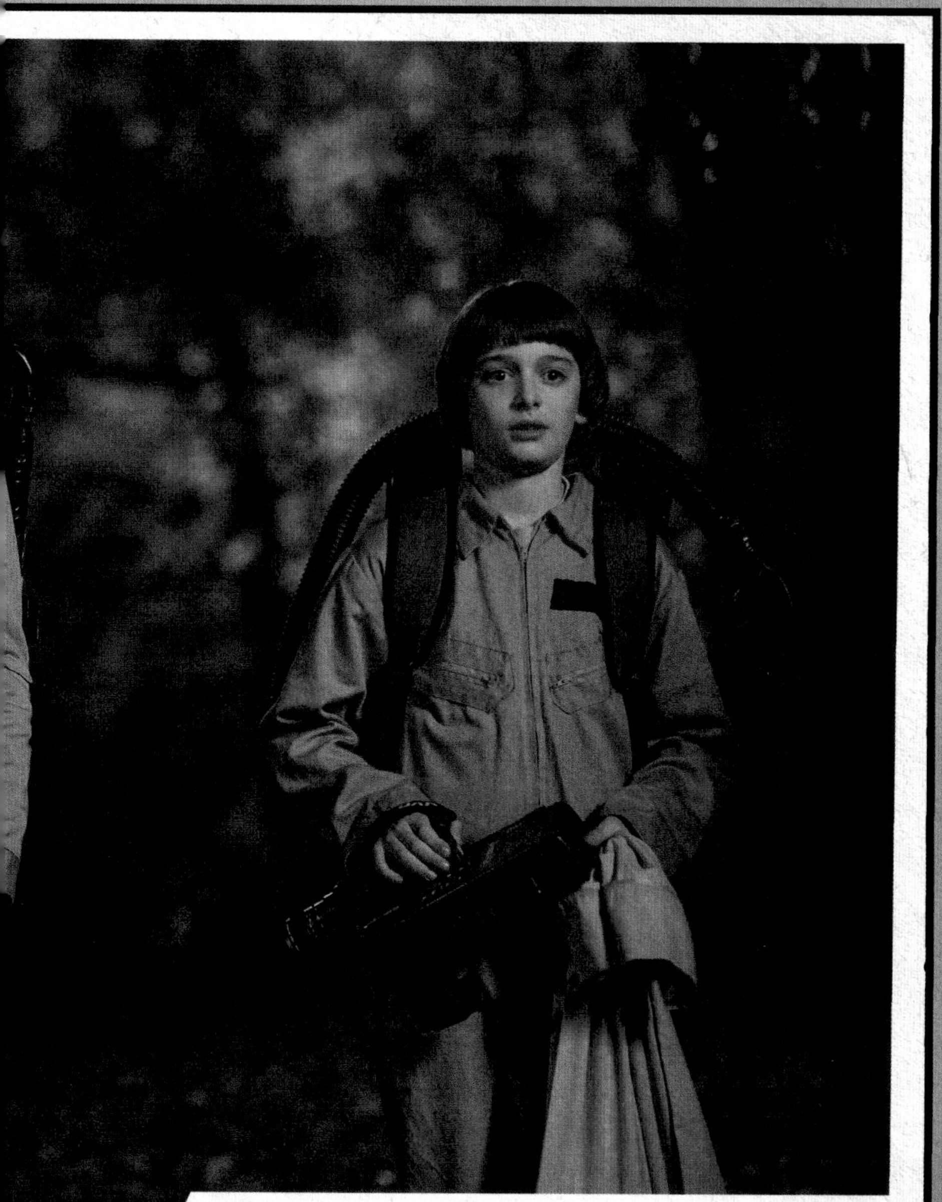

and discover your town has SECRETS.

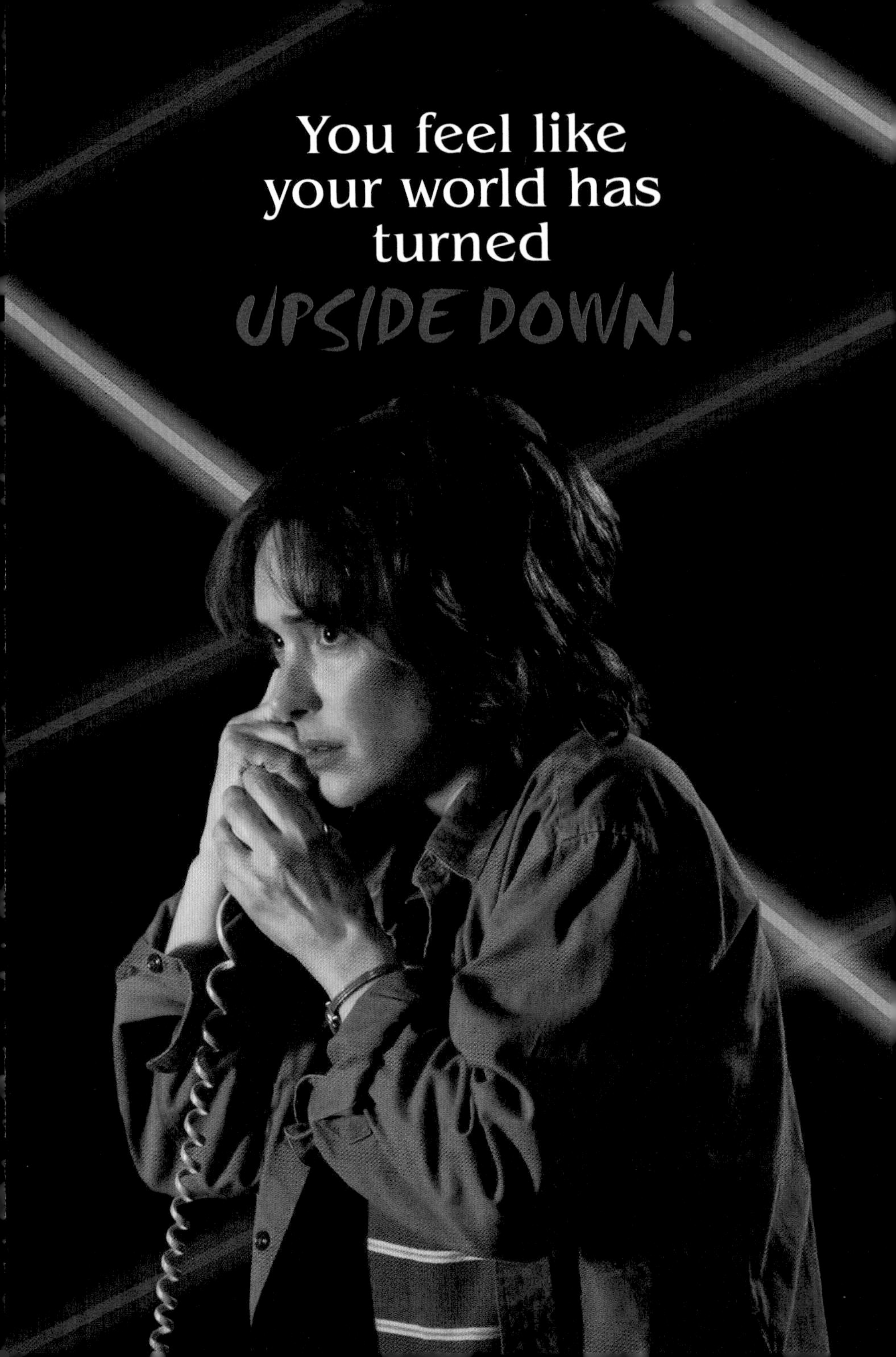
You feel like
your world has
turned
UPSIDE DOWN.

"I don't care
if anyone
believes me."

AT TIMES LIKE THIS,
IF YOU THINK
THERE'S SOMETHING
LURKING IN
THE DARK,
YOU'RE PROBABLY
RIGHT.

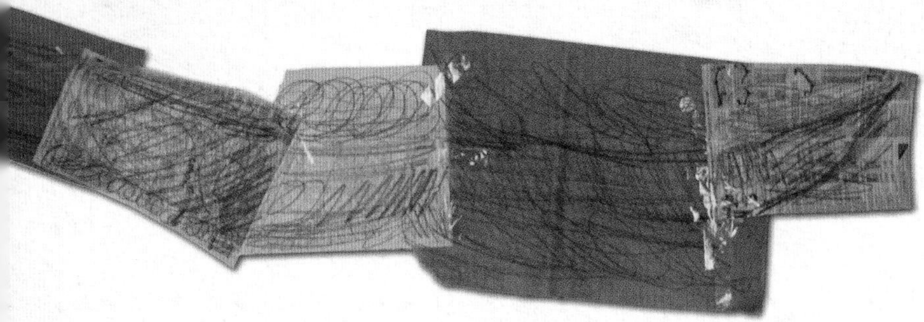

Don't be scared of
SHADOWS . . .

unless they're
SHADOW
MONSTERS.

It's time to get stealthy, like a ninja.

(And carrying a baseball bat studded with nails isn't a bad idea, either.)

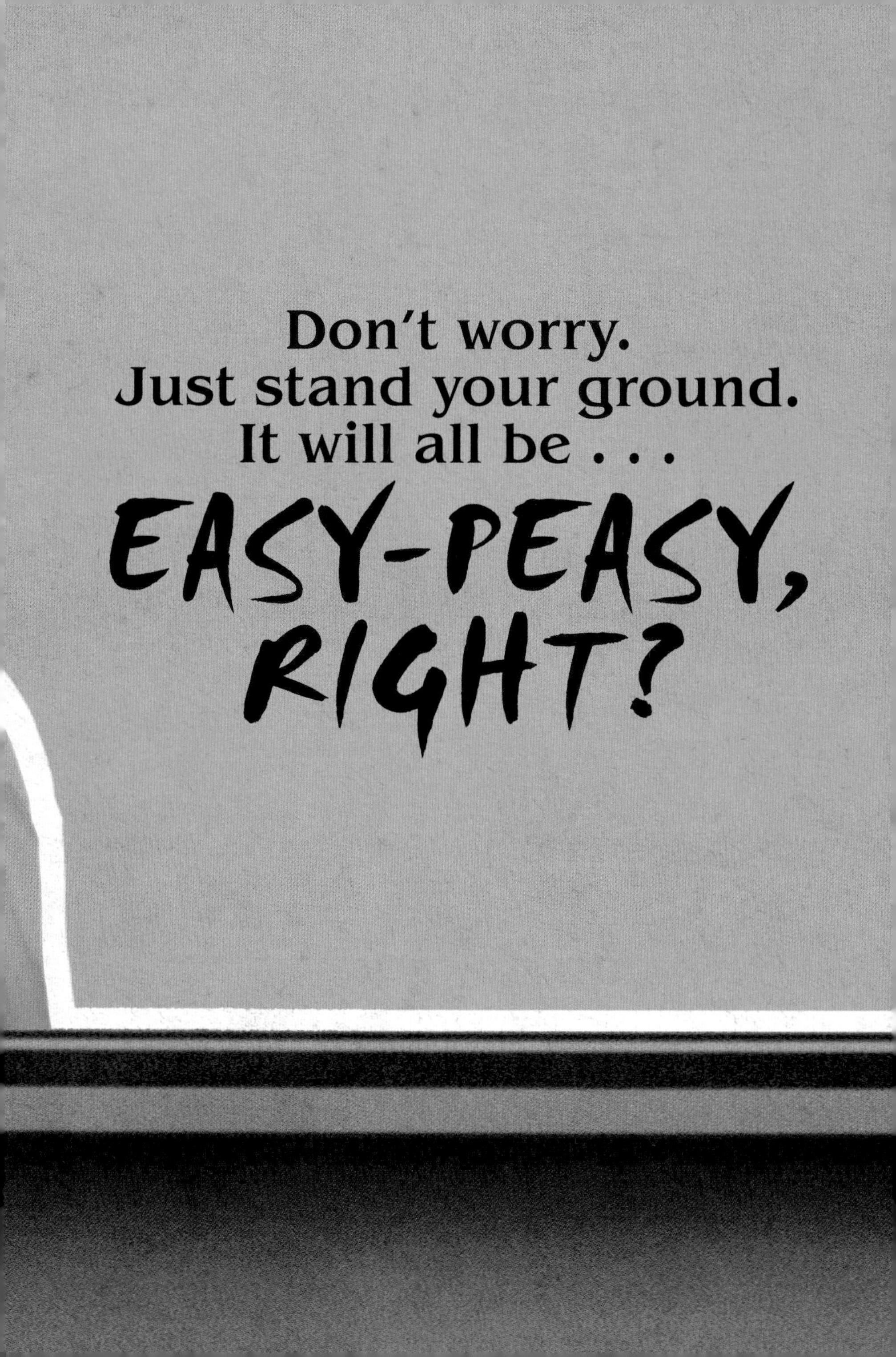
Don't worry.
Just stand your ground.
It will all be . . .
EASY-PEASY,
RIGHT?

You can ask your doctor to help.

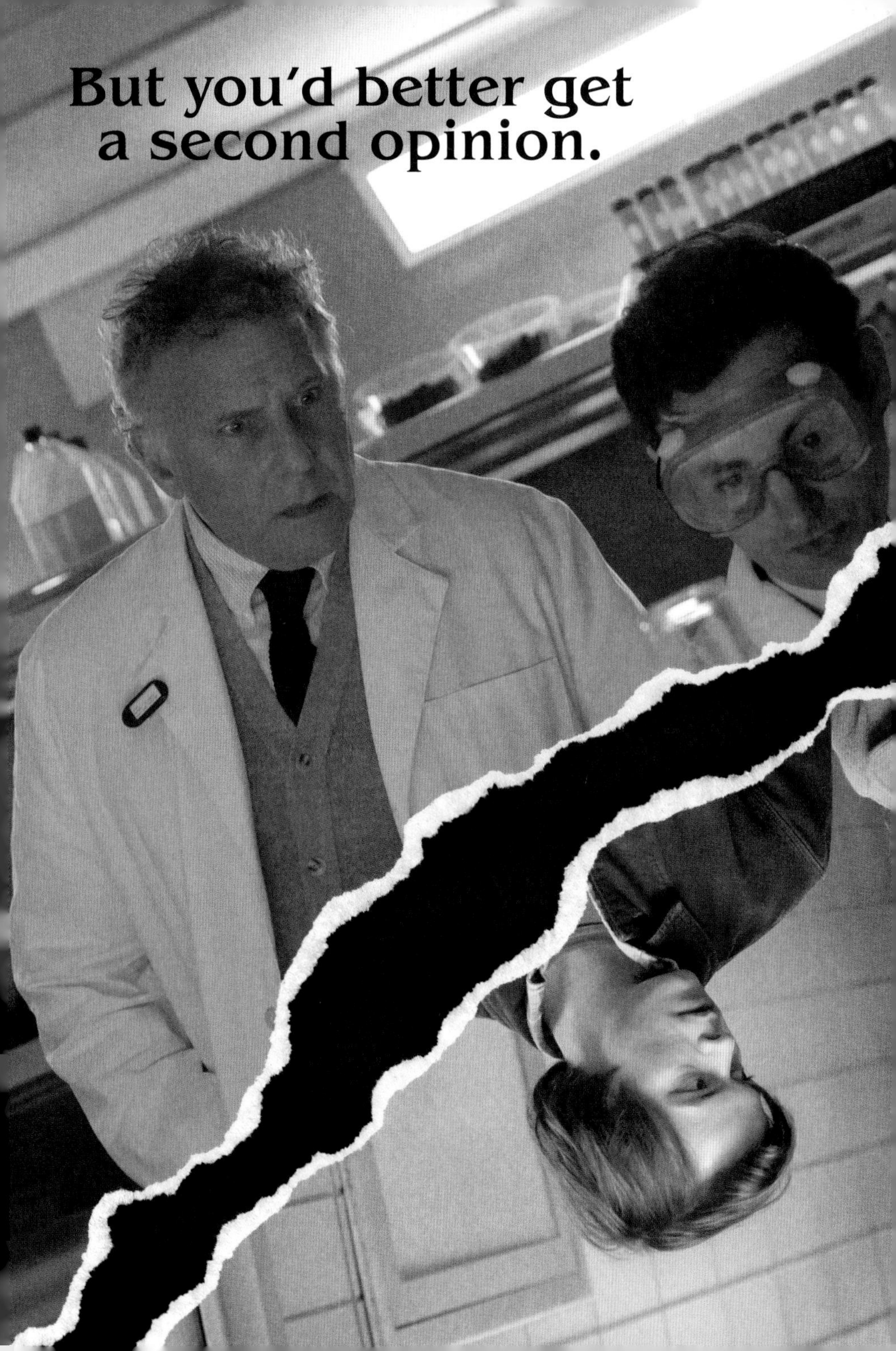

But you'd better get a second opinion.

Don't be stupid.
Follow the rules.

RULE 1

Always keep the curtains drawn.

RULE 2

Only open the door if you hear my secret knock

RULE 3

Never ever go outside alone especially not in daylight.

“SCIENCE IS NEAT,

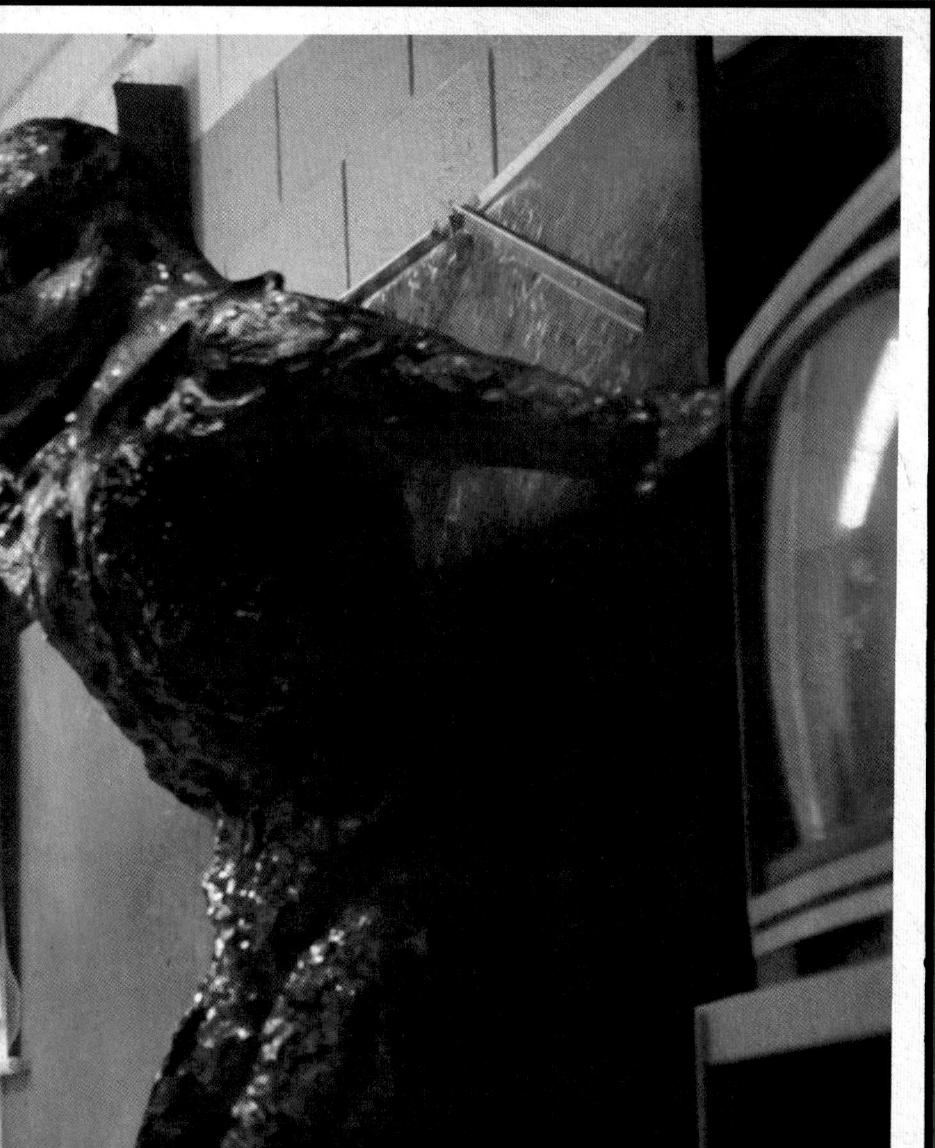

but I'm afraid it's
not very forgiving."

And when
you're certain
things can't get any
DARKER . . .

that's
your cue to
LIGHT
IT
UP.

HAWKINS

Be unstoppable.

FACE YOUR DEMONS.
LITERALLY.
THEN CRUSH THEM.

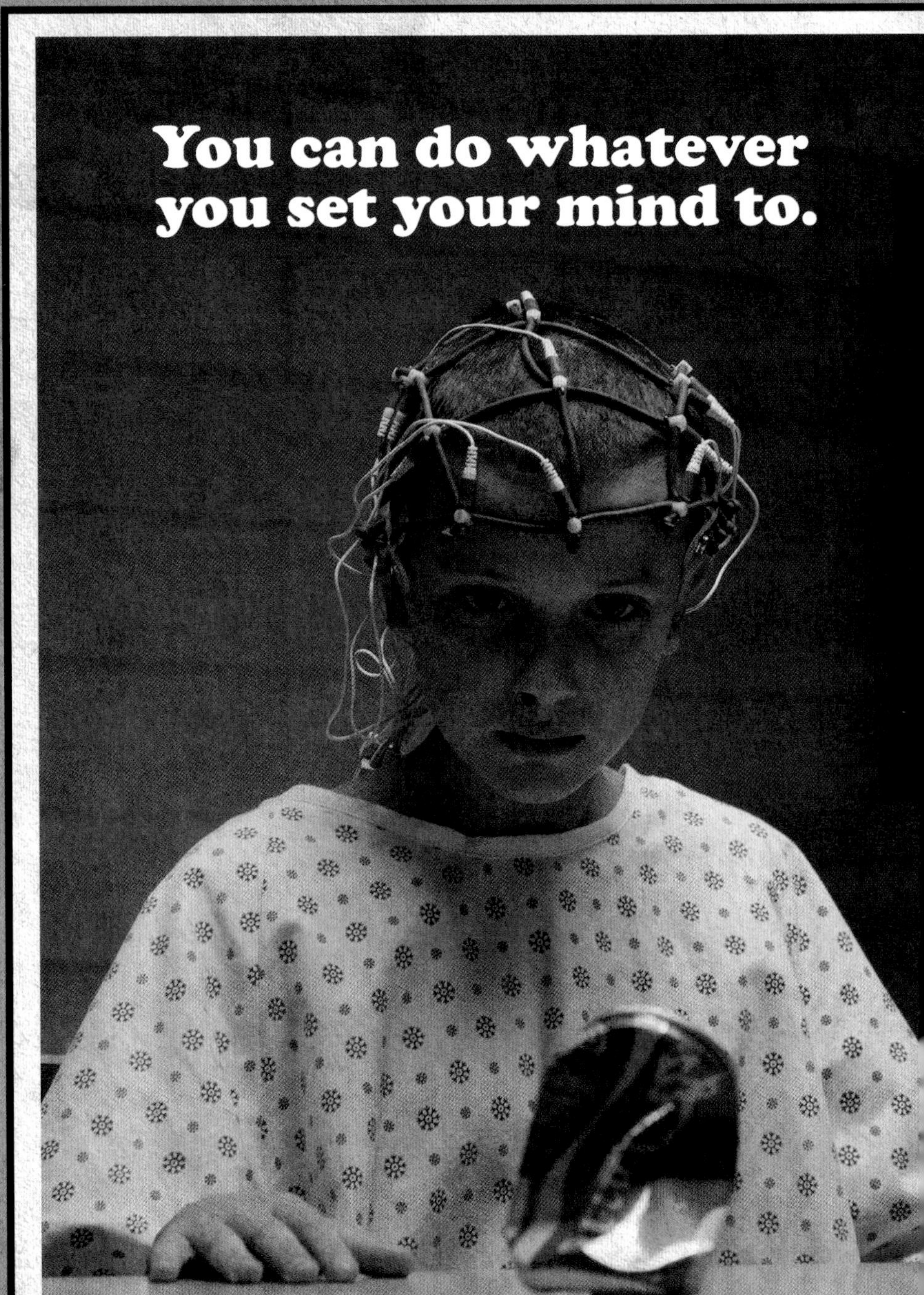
You can do whatever
you set your mind to.

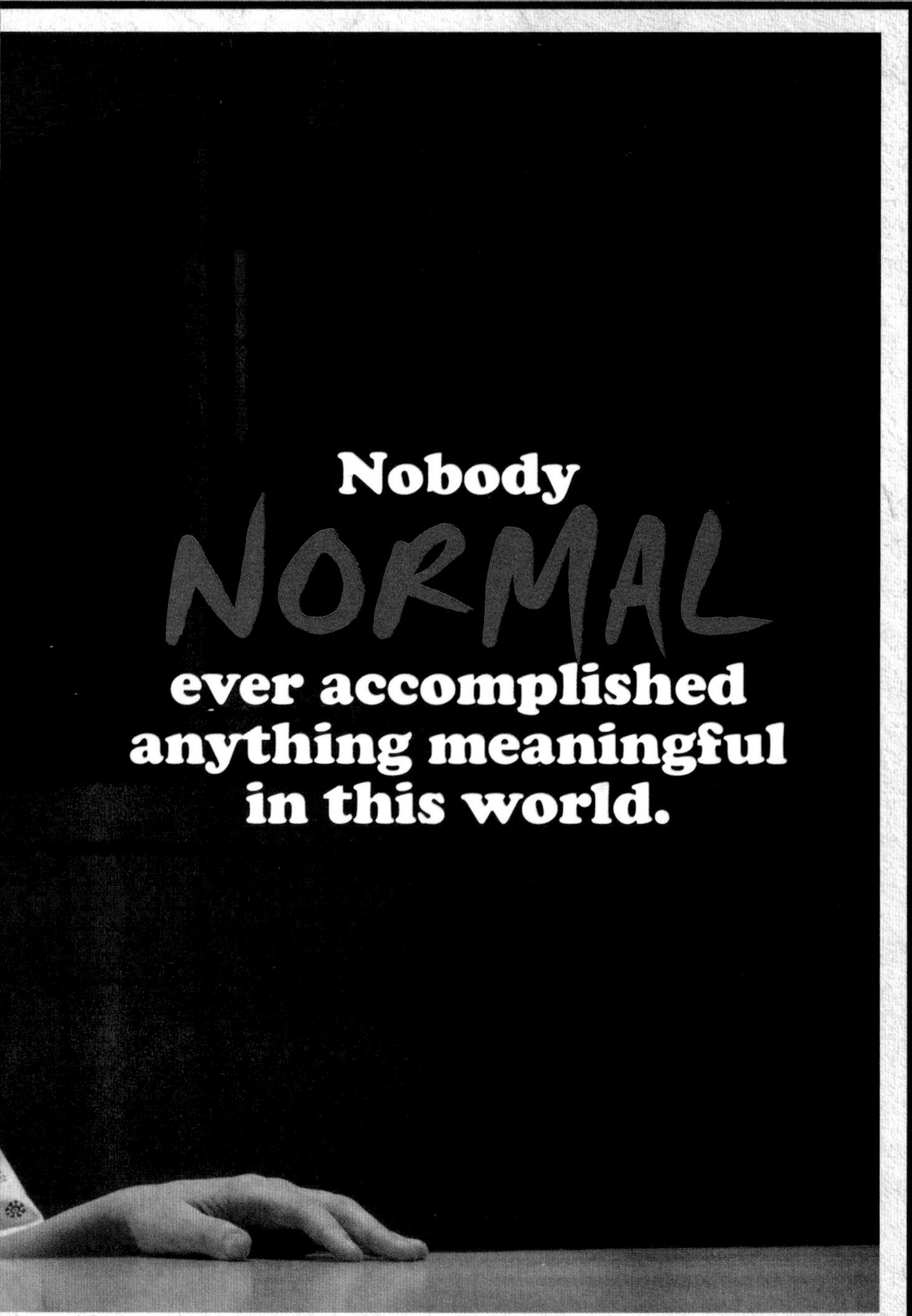
Nobody
NORMAL
ever accomplished
anything meaningful
in this world.

GATES ARE MEANT
TO BE CRASHED.
THE BIGGER
AND CREEPIER,
THE BETTER.

"Just be careful, all right? I can't lose you again."

“You won’t lose me.”

HAPPY RETURNS

When it feels like the end is near, keep your friends close . . .

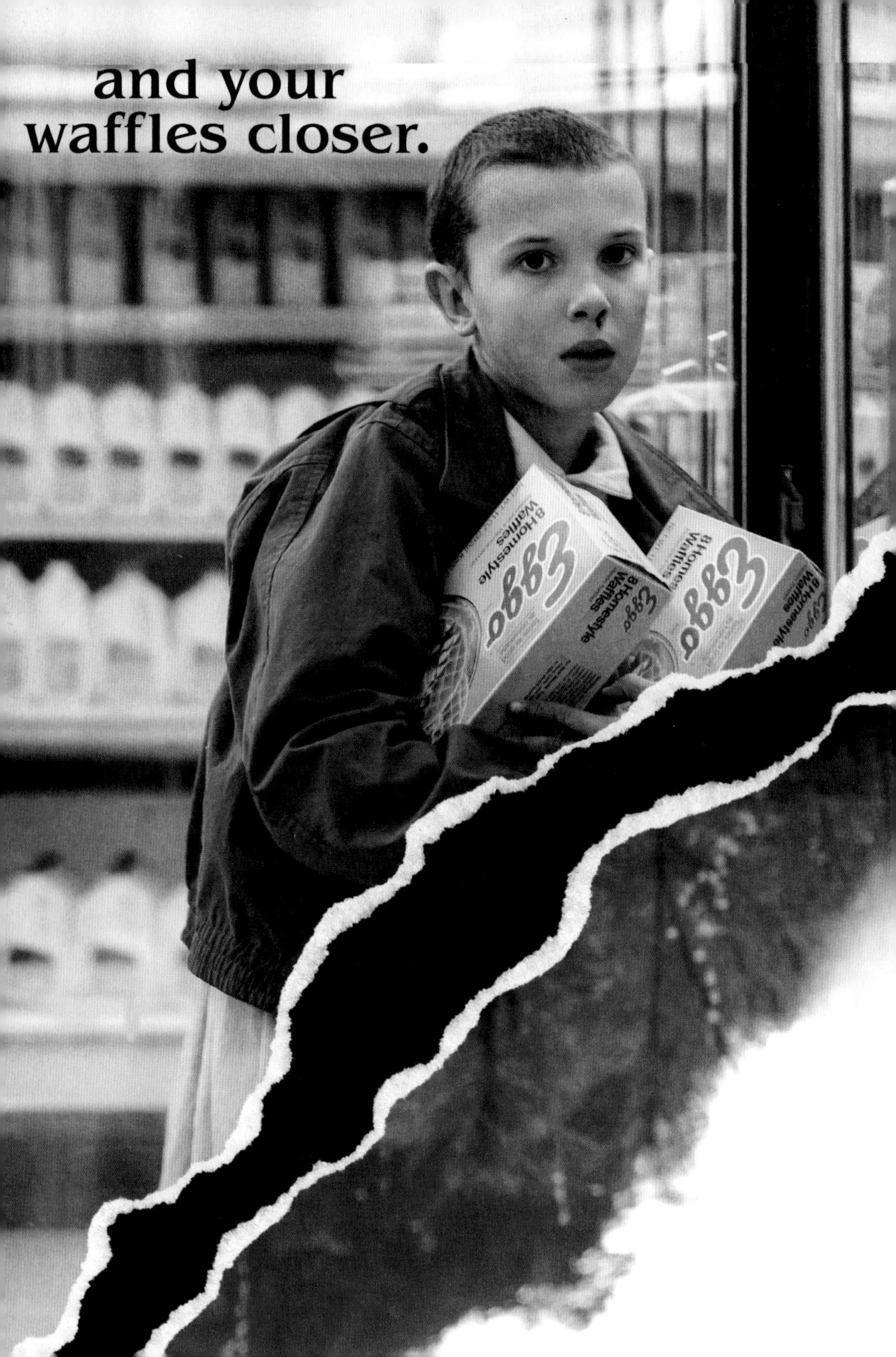
and your
waffles closer.
Eggo
8 Homestyle Waffles

Snow Ball 84

After you've
saved the world,
you deserve a party.

Though they may dance around it, sometimes friends are meant to be more than friends.

"Do you want to dance?"
"I don't know how."

“I don’t either. Do you want to figure it out?”

Nothing is gonna go
back to the way it was.
Not really.

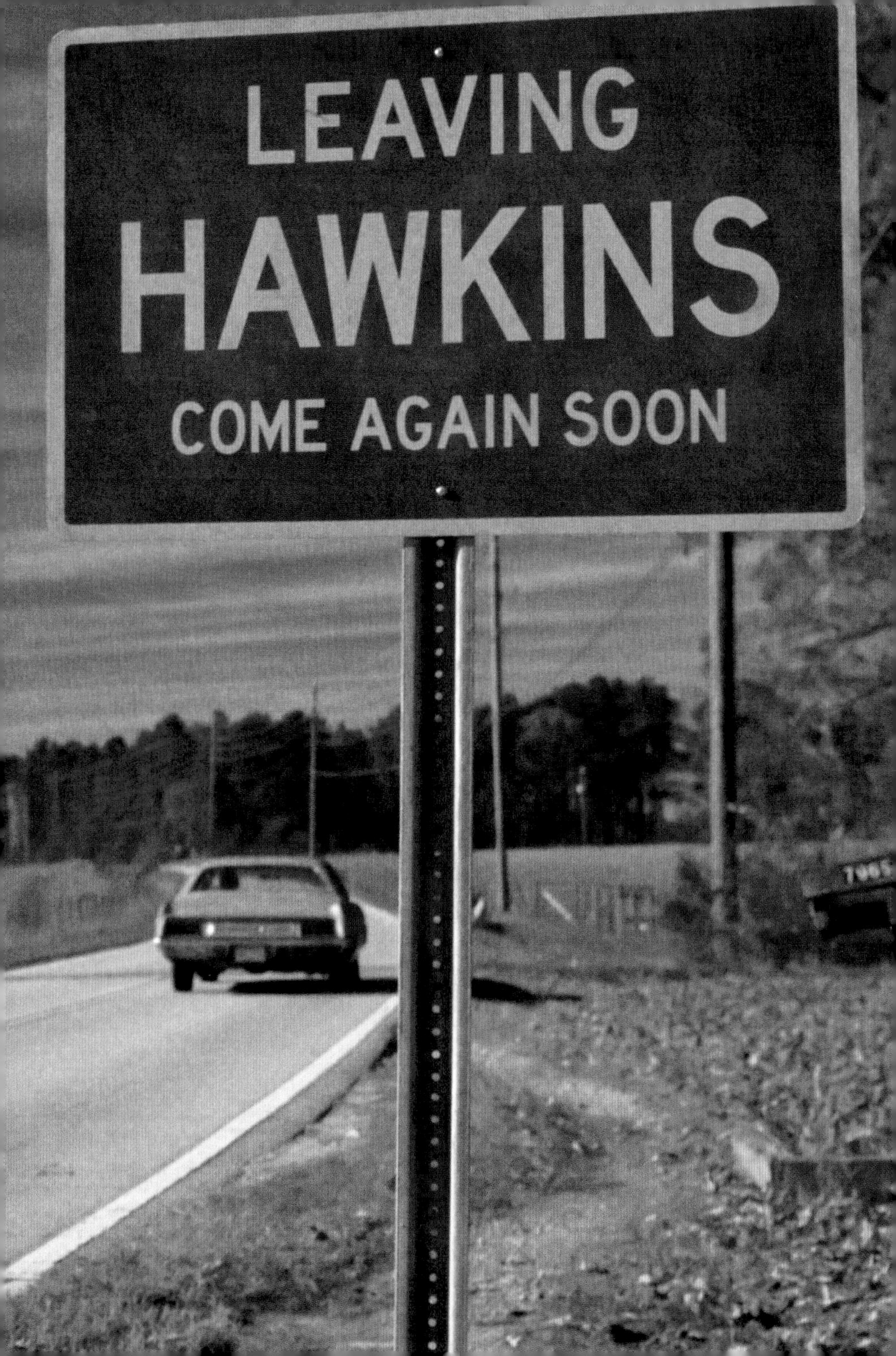
LEAVING
HAWKINS
COME AGAIN SOON

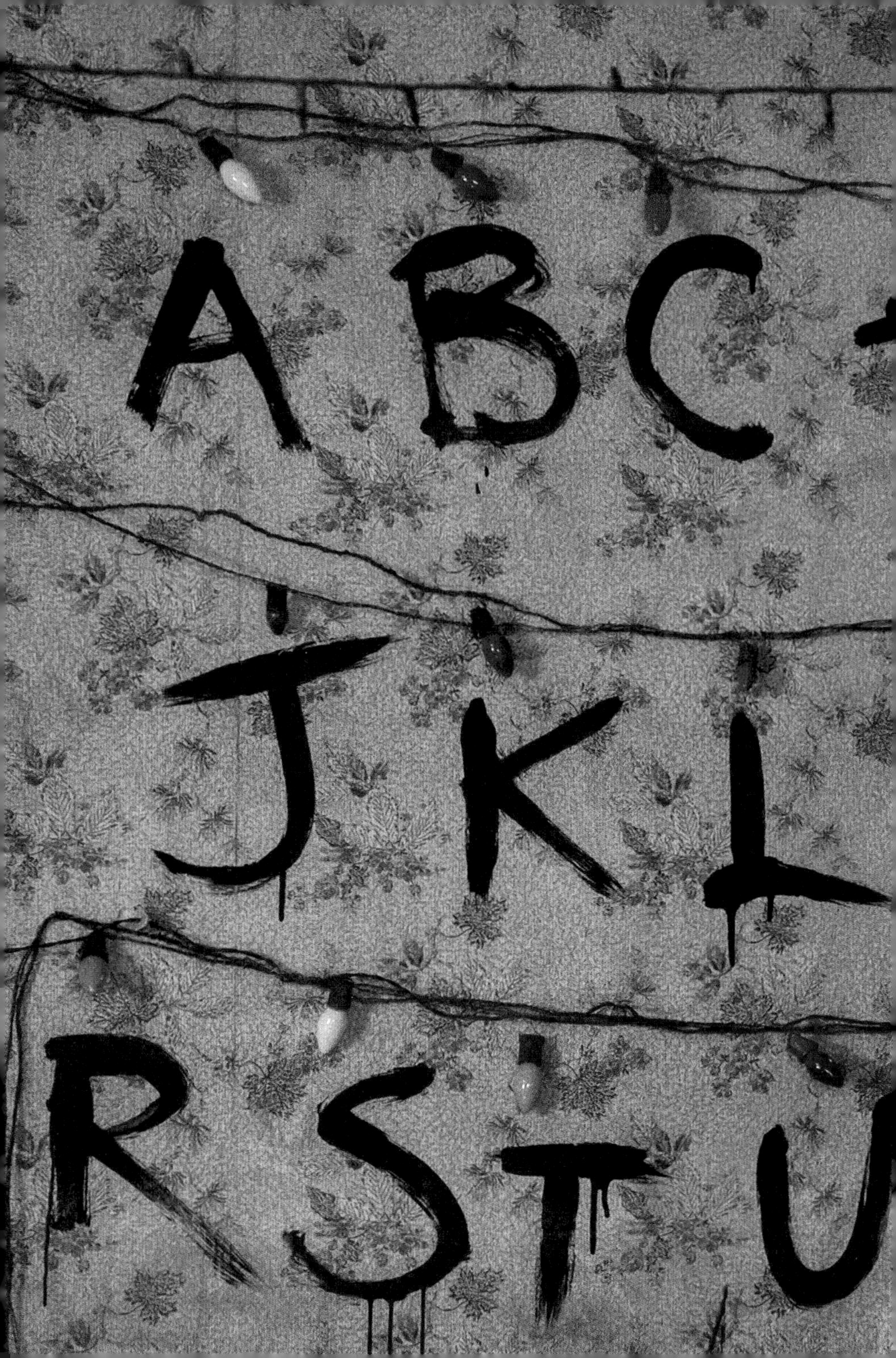
ABC
JKL
RSTU